❁ Contents ❁

Chapter 1
A great dog

Katie Woo's dog, Goldie,

was very old.

One day,
Goldie became
very ill. A week
later, she died.

Katie's mum
held Katie while
she cried.

"I will miss Goldie so much," Katie cried. "She was my best friend."

Katie's friend JoJo hugged

her. "I will miss Goldie too,"

said JoJo. "She was the nicest

dog in the world."

"She was!" agreed Pedro.

"Goldie loved running on the beach," said Pedro.

"We didn't have to go into the sea to get wet," said JoJo. "Goldie would just shake her fur and make us all wet!"

"Goldie was great in the snow, too!" said Pedro. "We used to throw snowballs and she would try to catch them in her mouth."

Chapter 2

A wagging tail

"Tell me some more happy stories about Goldie," said Katie.

JoJo grinned. "That's easy! There are so many."

"At Easter, Goldie ate my chicken drumstick," JoJo said. "I turned around, and it was gone!"

"Goldie was clever," said Katie. "And fast!"

"Goldie was so much fun
at Halloween," said Katie.
"Remember the time she
wore a badger costume? She
ran around and scared all
the other dogs!"

"Goldie loved

tickling my face

with her tail,"

said JoJo.

"She dusted the table with

it too," joked Katie's mum.

"And my computer!"

added Katie's dad.

"Her tail hardly ever

stopped wagging," said Katie.

"Goldie and I were both scared of thunder," said Katie. "But

when we hugged, we both felt better."

"Goldie was a good cuddler," agreed Katie's mum.

Katie's dad showed her

a photo. It was taken when

she and Goldie were little.

They were eating hot dogs

together.

"This photo is great,"

Katie said. "I love looking

at it."

Chapter 3
The scrapbook

JoJo had an idea. "We should make Katie a Goldie scrapbook. She can look at it whenever she feels sad."

Katie's mum found two photos of Goldie and Katie. In one, they were playing catch with a ball.

In the other, they were both very small. They were having a nap on the grass.

Katie drew a picture of

Goldie catching popcorn in

her mouth.

"She was good at that!"

Katie said, smiling. "She

never missed!"

"Goldie could skip too," said JoJo. "And kick a soccer ball!"

"And almost catch squirrels!" added Pedro.

"Goldie lived a long and

happy life," said Katie's mum.

"Yes, she did," said Katie.

That night at
bedtime, Katie
held Goldie's
picture and kissed it
goodnight.

"Goldie, I will always remember you," Katie promised.

And she always did.

About the author

Fran Manushkin is the author of many popular picture books, including *Baby, Come Out!*; *Latkes and Applesauce: A Hanukkah Story*; *The Belly Book* and *Big Girl Panties*. There is a real Katie Woo - she's Fran's great-niece - but she never gets in half the trouble that Katie Woo does in the books. Fran writes on her beloved Mac computer in New York City, USA, without the help of her two naughty cats, Chaim and Goldy.

About the illustrator

Tammie Lyon began her love for drawing at a young age while sitting at the kitchen table with her dad. She continued her love of art and eventually attended college, where she earned a bachelors degree in fine art. After a brief career as a professional ballet dancer, she decided to devote herself full time to illustration. Today she lives with her husband, Lee, in Cincinnati, Ohio, USA. Her dogs, Gus and Dudley, keep her company as she works in her studio.

✿ Glossary ✿

computer a machine that can store large amounts of information

costume clothes worn to look like someone or something else

cuddler someone who gives another person cuddles to comfort them

scrapbook a book with blank pages that hold pictures and other items you wish to keep

thunder the loud, booming sound that comes after a flash of lightning

❀ Discussion questions ❀

1. Have you ever had to say goodbye to someone? How did you feel?

2. The book lists many things Goldie liked to do. What other things do dogs like to do?

3. If you could have any kind of pet, what kind of pet would you choose?

❀ Writing prompts ❀

1. Goldie was Katie's best friend. What sort of things do you do with your friends? Make a list.

2. Goldie dressed up like a badger for Halloween. Think of another costume for Goldie and draw a picture of her in it. Write a sentence to explain why it would make a good costume for Goldie.

3. Katie remembers Goldie with a scrapbook. Another way to remember something is to write about it in a diary. Start your own diary, and write about something you want to remember.

Having fun with Katie Woo

In *Goodbye to Goldie*, Katie and her friends make a scrapbook that is all about her dog, Goldie. Make your own scrapbook page. Here's how:

1. Gather your supplies

You will need a piece of paper, crayons, felt tips, a glue stick, photos, stickers and anything else you want to use to decorate your page. Any type of paper will work, but if you want your page to last forever, ask an adult for some acid-free paper.

2. Choose a theme

What will your page be about? A grandparent, a favourite book, or a family holiday all make fun themes.

3. Get to work

Choose which photos you want to include. Do you want to include captions to describe your photos? What about some stickers? Before you glue anything down, lay your items out on your page to see how they fit. Then use your glue to stick them down.

Once your page is finished you can put it in an album. Then you can add more pages and build a whole scrapbook. Or treat your page as a work of art and hang it up for all to see!